FINN
the FORTUNATE
TIGERSHARK
& his FANTASTIC
FRIENDS

GEORGINA STEVENS
illustrations by TOM BAKER

I'm Clawdia, look out for me!

Finn was a curious tiger shark pup
Who lived on a reef in the sea
He adored nothing more than to play and explore
Finding treasures before eating tea

He came across bicycles, boats and some boots
A caravan, car and canoe
Gondolas, golf clubs and gleaming gold bars
And a sunken old submarine too

Can you find all of the items amongst the coral?

He especially loved finding presents that made
All his friends and his family snigger
Harry the hammerhead jumped when he saw
His glasses made everything...

BIGGER!

A bushy moustache
made a Whale Shark named Wilf
Laugh to himself every day

And a set of false-teeth
brought a smile to the face
Of Martha the old Manta Ray

Tee hee hee

While searching the seas to gather these gifts
His hunger grew out of control
So he greedily gobbled up snacks on his way
And sometimes he swallowed them...

WHOLE

He was seaweed with knobbles, he'd chew through a mile!
Then slurp up the bendy white sticks

BURP!

SLURP!

NOM NOM NOM NOM NOM NOM NOM !!!

He loved to eat crinkly old jelly fish yet
His favourite was blue pick and mix

What is a shark's favourite sandwich filling?
Peanut butter and jellyfish!

One day after eating a stack of these sweets
His stomach was starting to swell
It grumbled and mumbled, it moaned and it groaned
He was really not feeling that well

So his dad took him straight to the doctor
Where an x-ray was done double-quick
And what a surprise when they looked there, inside!
No wonder that Finn felt so sick!

DR WHITE

Oh dear, Finn looks a little green around the gills...

They saw carrier bags and the brightest blue lids
Utensils and rusty old tins
Five water bottles and two red balloons
A toothbrush and three swimming fins

A small fishing net and four coffee cups,
Can rings and seven containers
Some long bendy straws and six yoghurt pots
And an old pair of size thirteen trainers

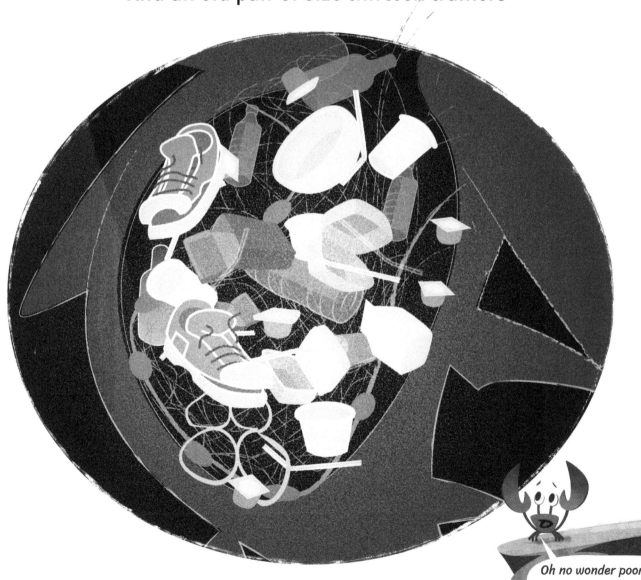

"What have you eaten?" the doctor exclaimed
"Plastic is bad for your tummy."
"But I thought it was just fish," poor Finn loudly wailed
"Because it looked tasty and yummy."

The news spread like plankton across the whole reef
And everyone knew of his plight
They were shocked when they heard what had made him so ill
And they promised to help put things right

The fish all agreed as to what must be done
And Tessa the Turtle delivered a speech
They collected the litter and put it in nets
And launched it right back to the beach

When people discovered the rubbish piled high
They flocked to the shore in distress

Ashamed and embarrassed about what they saw
They cried, "We MUST clean up this MESS"

So the people recycled their bottles
Creating smart clothes and new boats
The fishing nets magically turned into carpets
And also some beautiful coats

The foam cups were made into surfboards
And the cars and the bikes were all mended
The trainers became a new running track
The results, in the end, were quite splendid!

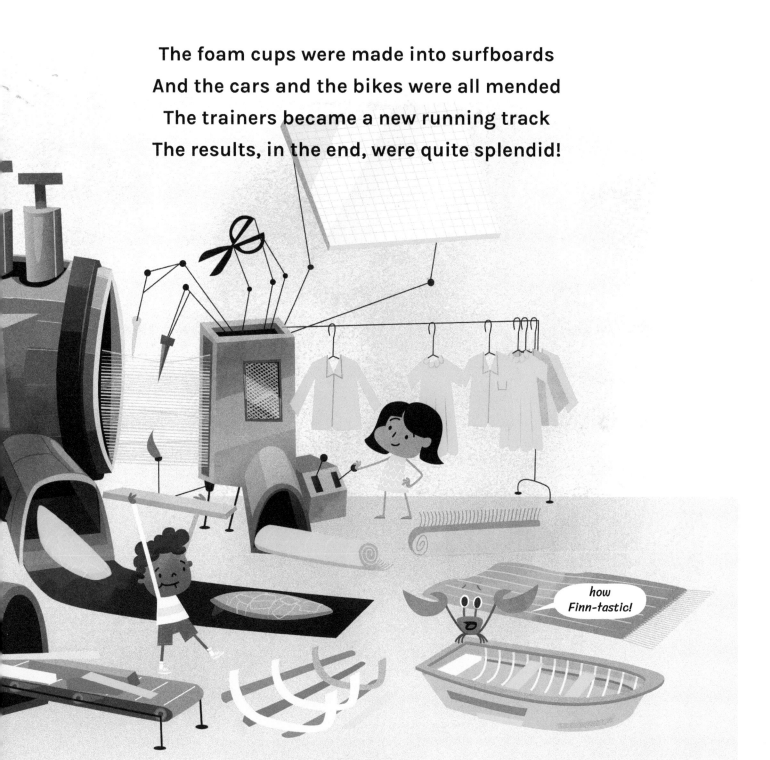

They promised to stick to reusable cups
Bottles and forks, knives and spoons
And to care for the fish and the birds they agreed
That they wouldn't let go of balloons

They'd refuse all the plastic containers and straws
At restaurants and cafés and delis
And their shopping bags, made out of canvas and cotton
Would never end up in fish bellies

What kind of whale can fly? A pilot whale

Instead of collecting seashells on the shore

They pick up the plastic instead

And beach-party clean ups
are held every year

So the fish aren't mistakenly fed

The people have cautioned and
warned all their friends

not even here

'fraid not

Most plastic will never decay

this is still
not away

Our rubbish will always go
somewhere on Earth

There is

NO

such place as

AWAY

there really
is no away

And even though Finn's feeling much better now
We can all stop his friends getting ill
By making sure plastic stays out of the sea
Or we'll risk losing whales down to krill

Our seas and their creatures are part of the web
Of life on which all things depend

By working altogether
we can save this world

Let's do it for
Finn and his friends.

The cast

Finn the Tiger Shark

Tiger Sharks really do like to eat almost anything they find! Whilst Finn was very fortunate, many different sharks, fish, mammals and birds are being hurt by plastic that gets in our oceans. And when plastic has been in the sea for a long time, it even starts to smell and look like food to our ocean friends. Plastic bags also look a lot like jelly fish when they are in the sea, and are mistakenly eaten by many fish. So next time you go shopping, why not take a reusable shopping bag with you, instead of using a plastic one?

NEAR THREATENED

Harry the Hammerhead Shark

Hammerheads do not eat as much rubbish as Tiger Sharks, but they are endangered because their fins are used in a lot of products. So if you are eating soup at a restaurant, make sure it doesn't contain a shark fin – they don't taste of anything and sharks really need their fins to swim! And next time someone you know buys a moisturiser or cosmetics, check that they do not contain squalene, which is made from shark liver oil. Sharks need their livers too and there are plenty of other much nicer things we can put in those products which do not hurt our ocean friends.

ENDANGERED

Squalene? You must be squidding?

Wilf the Whale Shark

The Whale Shark is the largest living fish on the planet. And they also have very large mouths! When they feed, they swim around with their enormous mouths open to catch tiny little animals called algae and plankton, which they think are delicious. Unfortunately, this also means that they eat a lot of plastic by mistake, which can be very bad for them. Why not get involved in a fun beach clean-up near you to help reduce the amount of plastic these amazing creatures might swallow?

Martha the Manta Ray

Martha probably came up with the idea to send all the plastic back to the shore to show the people what they were doing, because Manta Rays are the cleverest of all fish! However, they are also filter feeders, just like Wilf the Whale shark, and so they also eat a lot of plastic by mistake when they swim around with their mouths open. Next time you have a drink when you are at a cafe, make sure to ask for no plastic straw, because many straws find their way into our oceans.

Dr Greta White the Great White Shark

Great White Sharks look scary don't they!? But they're not! They are just big fish, who eat other fish. It's what they do. And by eating other fish, who in turn, eat other fish, who eat other fish, they keep things balanced in the sea. But because so many humans also catch and eat a lot of fish, we have lost that balance. And sadly, many Great White Sharks also get caught in large fishing nets, which is why there are only about 3,500 of them left. We can help save these amazing animals by making sure the fish we eat is sourced sustainably, leaving enough fish in the ocean for everyone to eat.

ENDANGERED

 Look out for the Marine Stewardship Council blue fish logo when you go shopping or eat at a restaurant. **msc.org**

Coral Reef

Coral reefs are home to almost 25% of marine animals. They are amazingly beautiful and all the fish like to hang out close to them and some of the fish like to eat the coral too. However, corals are eating lots of tiny pieces of plastic, called microplastics, which get stuck in their stomachs (just like poor Finn). When they have a full tummy of plastic, they cannot fit in any of their proper food and so they get very hungry. You can stop the corals getting so hungry by making sure that your family's toothpaste and face washes do not contain microbeads, which are tiny pieces of plastic, which get into our oceans when we use them.

If you want to find out more ways you can help stem the tide of plastic pollution and save our oceans, and more about any of the ideas above, visit **www.bethechangebooks.org** and take a quick look at the A-Z at the back of this book.

Tessa the Green Sea Turtle

Half of all Sea Turtles in our oceans have eaten some sort of plastic or other rubbish, it is thought. And, like many of the other species here, some of them also get caught up in our plastic waste, which is partly why nearly all species of Sea Turtle are now endangered. If a Sea Turtle eats a balloon, it can stop them being able to swim down to the sea bed to eat their favourite algae or seagrass, which can leave them very hungry. So next time you have a party, why not use paper pinwheels instead?

ENDANGERED

VULNERABLE

Humans

Not only are we harming millions of animals and birds with the plastic we throw "away", we are also making ourselves poorly. The fish we eat is now likely to contain plastic, and so is the water we drink. So it makes sense for us to stop using single use plastics and anything that contains microbeads, doesn't it? Both for us and for the amazing creatures who also live on this planet. Why not write to a company whose products you like, with some ideas as to how they could make their products last longer or be better for our environment?

Plastic

Take a look around you and you will notice that a lot of your things are made of plastic. For some toys and other things, plastic is very useful, but half of all the plastic made each year is for things which are only used once and for a very short time, but then can take up to 1000 years to break down. Over 90% of seabirds worldwide have plastic pieces in their stomachs, which must make them feel very poorly. Why not see if you can live for a whole week without using single use plastic such as plastic bags, straws, bottles and cutlery? You might find some really fun things to use instead – if you do, please let us know!

ABUNDANT AND THRIVING

Your handy A–Z to help reduce Ocean Plastic

Action Figures in the ocean?! Yes! Lots of old toys end up there, so why not give your old action figures to your local charity shop or your younger friends? Or if they're broken, you can donate them to somewhere that will make them into new toys, such as toy-lab.com.

Balloons cannot be recycled and can harm animals if they eat them. Why not use paper ribbon dancers or pinwheels at your party instead? Balloons are so last year!

Clothes made from man-made fabrics shed microfibers when washed, which then get into our oceans and waterways, and harm the fish that eat them. Ask your parents to buy clothes made from natural materials such as wool, cotton and linen, or use a special bag to wash your clothes, such as the guppyfriend.com.

Disposable and single use plastic is everywhere! Say no to single use plastic straws, bags, cutlery and bottles when you are out and about. And say yes to taking your own lovely reusable water bottles, bags, containers and straws!

Earbuds that are flushed down the loo can end up in our oceans. Use ones with paper stems and put them in the bin or use a flannel instead! **Electric toys (and their batteries)** cannot go in the bin as they contain lots of nasty chemicals. Take them to a specialist centre to recycle or use rechargeable batteries and toys instead.

Food wrappers like crisp and chocolate packets cannot be recycled, so why not use them to make paper chains, or make your own crisps! And instead of non-recyclable cling film and foil on your sandwiches why not ask for a Tupperware box?

Glass is better! Much more glass gets recycled or reused than plastic, so next time you go shopping try to choose glass containers rather than plastic. It cannot blow into our waterways as easily as plastic, and it doesn't smell as good to fish so they don't eat it!

Head teachers cannot be recycled but they can help you inspire the rest of your school to ditch the plastic! Chat to them about whether you could put on an assembly about ocean plastic or get the school involved in a beach clean-up.

Inflatable toys and paddling pools aren't recyclable, so if they spring a leak, why not try to patch them up with a piece from another inflatable toy that you don't use anymore? It's easier than you think and stops them ending up in a big landfill site or worse, in the ocean.

Junk? You may not want that toy anymore, but someone will! There is always a home for everything, and your local charity shop can raise money from your unwanted toys, clothes and other things. And remember, there is no such place as away!

Know what you can recycle at home, and stick a poster on your recycling bin so that everyone else knows too. Make your recycling bin the biggest bin in your house and put it where it is easy for everyone to use. Make your landfill bin the smallest bin, and put it away in a cupboard, so everyone has to think before they throw anything away!

Lego is not recyclable, so make sure you give your old Lego pieces to a friend or to the charity shop, or make a piece of art with them.

Make and Mend as much as possible! You can have so much fun and learn so much when you make and mend things too. Ask your grandparents about this, they usually know about this stuff!

Nappies (or disposable diapers) can take up to 500 years to biodegrade and are largely unrecyclable. Lots have been found on beaches around the world, which isn't fun for anyone on the beach or the fish who swim with them! If you have a baby brother or sister, or know someone with a baby, why not suggest they try reusable nappies? They do need washing but they won't get in the sea!

Oil is a non-renewable fossil fuel made from the buried remains of plants and animals that lived millions of years ago. It is what plastic is made from. When used, it produces carbon dioxide which is contributing to climate change, but that's another story in the series.

Petitions can help to get things changed. You can sign petitions to tell politicians that you think they should change laws about plastic or other issues, or to tell companies that you want them to stop using so much plastic. You can even ask your parents to help you start your own petition.

Question whether you need anything new, especially if it's made of plastic, or if it won't last very long. It's annoying when things break, and then sit broken in a pile, so you can't see all of your good toys, right? So why not ask for something that will last for a long time instead.

Refuse all plastic straws and plastic cutlery when you go out to eat or drink! So many straws end up in the ocean and harm our wildlife.

Shoes can be given to charity shops if they are too small for you. Or if they are a bit worn out, send any old trainers, like the ones Finn ate, to Nike who will turn them into a new running track or a playground.

Plastic **Toothbrushes** are tricky to recycle, but a few companies who make them do take them back including Toothbrush Express and Colgate. So pop 'em in the post! It's better to have a wooden toothbrush or one with reusable parts though, and there are lots to choose from!

The **Underwater** world is home to an estimated 10 million different creatures! How cool is that? Get your snorkel on and go and have a look next time you are by the sea.

Volunteer to help clean up a beach near you with your family or with your school or club.

Write to a company and let them know if you think they could make a product better, make it last longer, make it from different recyclable materials or if you think they should make something else instead.

Xmas is a time of lots of presents, which is great! But it also means a lot of things are thrown away. Why not give all of your unwanted presents or old toys to a charity shop, and ask for no plastic presents this year?

Yoghurt is delicious and most yoghurt pots can be recycled, but check yours first, and then make sure all of your empty yoghurt pots go in the right recycling bin!

Zooplankton and phytoplankton are the smallest creatures that live in the ocean. They might be small but they are very important and they are at risk from plastic. So they asked me to say a **big thank you** to each and every one of you who are doing your bit to reduce plastic getting into the sea! Thank You.

For Rafael and all you Ocean Warriors